STAR WARS

EPISODE V
THE EMPIRE STRIKES BACK

BASED ON A STORY BY
GEORGE LUCAS

SCREENPLAY BY
LEIGH BRACKETT
AND
LAWRENCE KASDAN

HAMBURG • LONDON • LOS ANGELES • TOKYO

Editor - Rob Tokar
Contributing Editor - Jake Forbes
Graphic Designer and Letterer - Monalisa J. de Asis
Cover Designer - Raymond Makowski
Graphic Artists - Louis Csontos and John Lo

Digital Imaging Manager - Chris Buford
Pre-Press Manager - Antonio DePietro
Production Managers - Jennifer Miller and Mutsumi Miyazaki
Senior Designer - Anna Kernbaum
Art Director - Matt Alford
Senior Editor - Elizabeth Hurchalla
Managing Editor - Jill Freshney
VP of Production - Ron Klamert
Editor-in-Chief - Mike Kiley
President & C.O.O. - John Parker
Publisher & C.E.O. - Stuart Levy

E-mail: info@tokyopop.com
Come visit us online at www.TOKYOPOP.com

A ☺TOKYOPOP® Cine-Manga® Book
TOKYOPOP Inc.
5900 Wilshire Blvd., Suite 2000
Los Angeles, CA 90036

Star Wars: The Empire Strikes Back

Special thanks to Paul Southern, Amy Gary,
Sue Rostoni and Valentina Dose.

ISBN: 1-59532-896-3

First TOKYOPOP® printing: May 2005

10 9 8 7 6 5 4 3 2 1

Printed in China

LUKE SKYWALKER:
FARM BOY TURNED
REBEL COMMANDER

DARTH VADER:
LORD OF THE SITH

CHEWBACCA:
WOOKIEE AND
HAN SOLO'S PARTNER

HAN SOLO:
SMUGGLER

SEE-THREEPIO (C-3PO):
PROTOCOL DROID

LEIA ORGANA:
PRINCESS AND
REBEL LEADER

ARTOO-DETOO (R2-D2):
ASTROMECH DROID
AND SEE-THREEPIO'S
SIDEKICK

OBI-WAN KENOBI:
DECEASED JEDI
MASTER

A long time ago in a galaxy far, far away....

It is a dark time for the Rebellion. Although the Death Star has been destroyed, Imperial troops have driven the Rebel forces from their hidden base and pursued them across the galaxy.

Evading the dreaded Imperial Starfleet, a group of freedom fighters led by Luke Skywalker has established a new secret base on the remote ice world of Hoth.

The evil lord Darth Vader, obsessed with finding young Skywalker, has dispatched thousands of remote probes into the far reaches of space....

AS THE SMOKE CLEARS, AN IMPERIAL PROBE DROID EMERGES AND BEGINS ITS SEARCH.

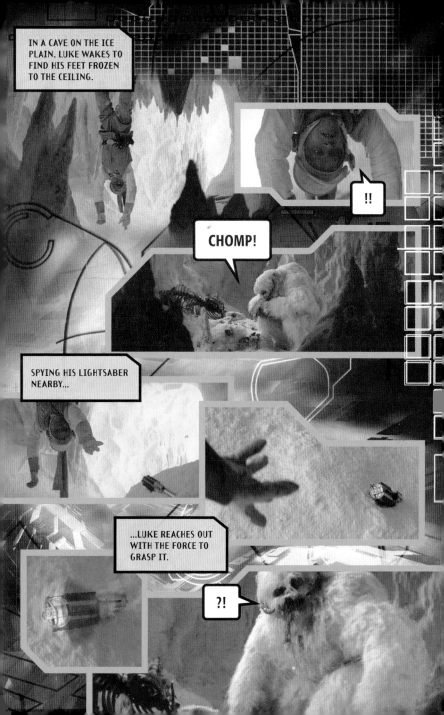

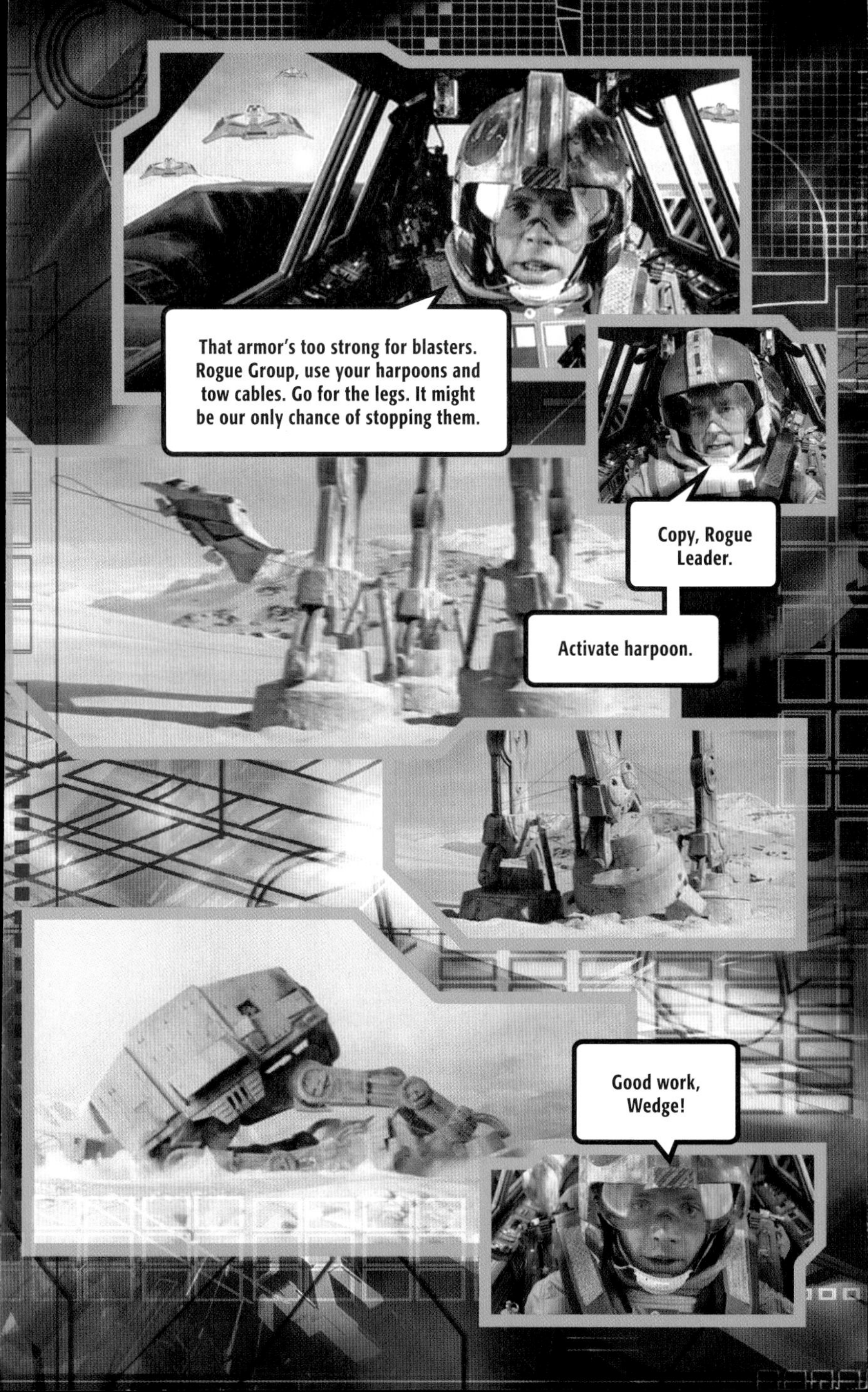
That armor's too strong for blasters. Rogue Group, use your harpoons and tow cables. Go for the legs. It might be our only chance of stopping them.
Copy, Rogue Leader.
Activate harpoon.
Good work, Wedge!

Star Destroyers, two of them, coming right at us.
Prepare to make the jump to light speed!
BUT, SIR! I NOTICED EARLIER THAT THE HYPERDRIVE MOTIVATOR HAS BEEN DAMAGED. IT'S IMPOSSIBLE TO GO TO LIGHT SPEED!
I think we're in trouble.
Asteroids!

What are you doing? You're not actually going into an asteroid field?
They'd be crazy to follow us, wouldn't they?
SIR, THE POSSIBILITY OF SUCCESSFULLY NAVIGATING AN ASTEROID FIELD IS APPROXIMATELY THREE THOUSAND, SEVEN HUNDRED AND TWENTY TO ONE!
Never tell me the odds!

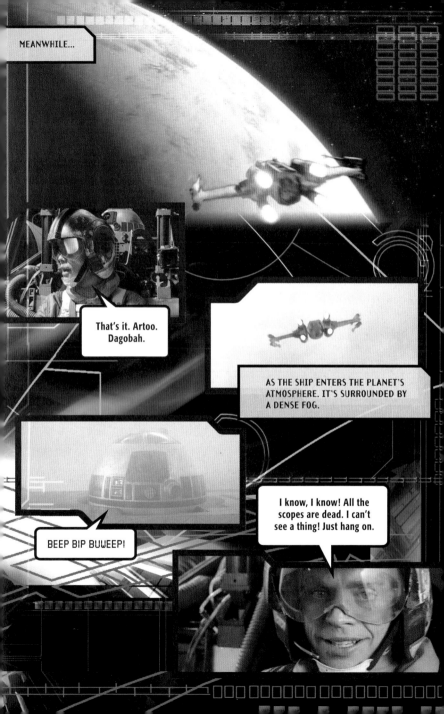

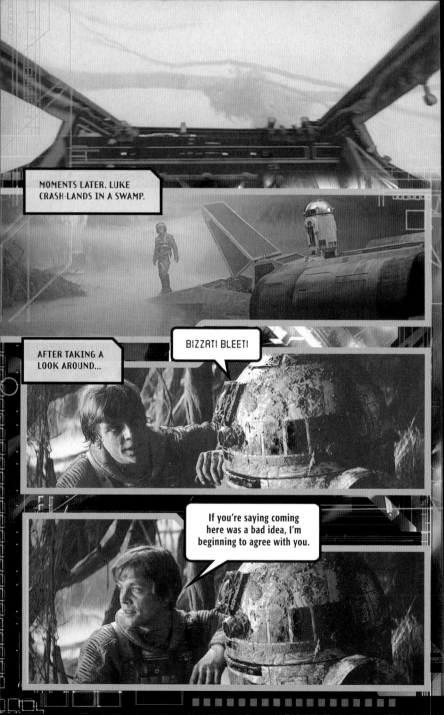

MEANWHILE, ON THE MILLENNIUM FALCON...
SIR, IT'S QUITE POSSIBLE THIS ASTEROID IS NOT ENTIRELY STABLE.
Not entirely stable? I'm glad you're here to tell us these things, professor.
Let go.
Don't get excited.
Captain, being held by you isn't quite enough to get me excited.
Sorry, sweetheart. We haven't got time for anything else.

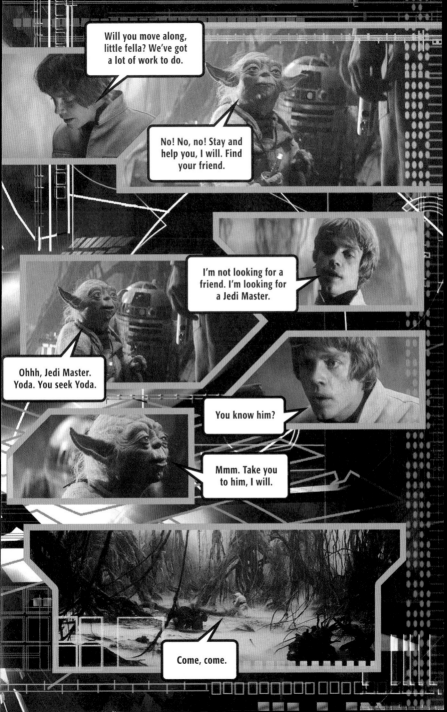

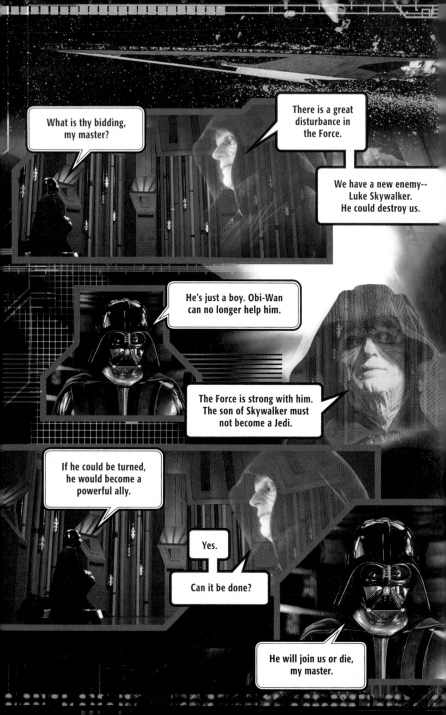

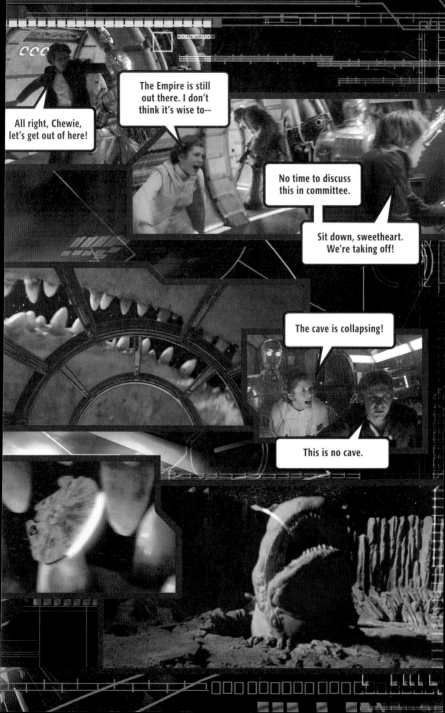

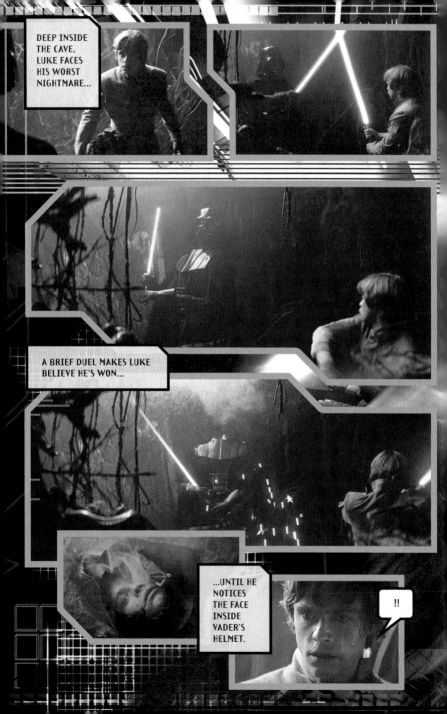

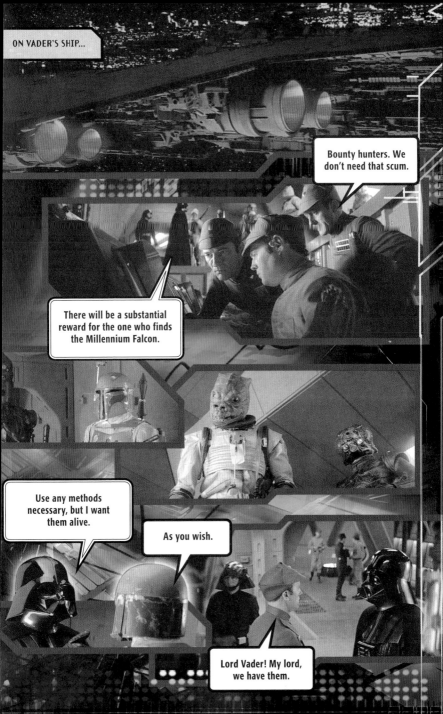

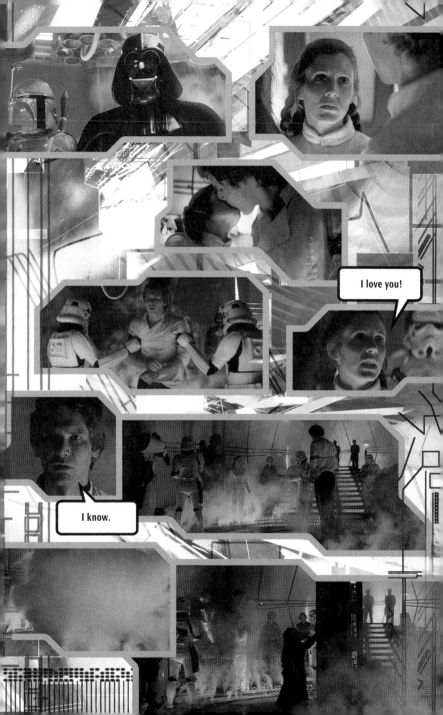

SOON...

VADER USES THE FORCE TO BOMBARD LUKE WITH HEAVY OBJECTS, KNOCKING LUKE INTO A REACTOR SHAFT.

IN CLOUD CITY'S REACTOR CORE. THE LIGHTSABER BATTLE CONTINUES...

AS THE MEDICAL DROID TESTS LUKE'S MECHANICAL HAND...

...THE MILLENNIUM FALCON GOES OFF IN SEARCH OF ITS CAPTAIN.

DENGAR
Dengar is a grizzled human bounty hunter who hails from Correllia, Han Solo's home planet. His ship is the Punishing One, a Corellian Jumpmaster 5000.

ZUCKUSS
Zuckuss is an insectoid bounty hunter of few words. He is a short, stocky being with a grubby robe, and a number of breather tanks affixed to his head. He hails from the planet Gand and his ship is the Mist Hunter.

BOSSK
Bossk is a towering reptilian humanoid and skilled predator from the planet Trandosha, with keen hearing and lethal claws.

IG-88
After the destruction caused by the legions of mechanized troops used by the Trade Federation, legislation was passed outlawing combat droids. Relics from that era still exist, such as the battered chrome war droid known as IG-88. Built at Holowan Laboratories, IG-88 is a longtime rival of Boba Fett's. His ship is the IG-2000.

BOBA FETT
Boba Fett is the cloned child of Jango Fett, who watched his father die at the hands of Jedi at the outbreak of the Clone Wars. During the time of the Empire, Boba Fett emerged as the preeminent bounty hunter of the galaxy. Boba Fett's armor, like his father's, is a battered, weapon-covered spacesuit equipped with a rocketpack. His gauntlets contain a flamethrower and a whipcord lanyard launcher. His kneepads conceal rocket dart launchers. Several ominous braids hang from his shoulder-- trophies from fallen prey--that underscore this hunter's lethality. He pilots his father's ship, the Slave 1.

BOUNTY HUNTERS

CREATURES AND ALIENS

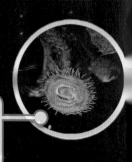

MYNOCK
Leathery-winged manta-like flyers, mynocks are a common pest faced by space travelers. The parasitic creatures attach themselves to hosts via their bristly suction cup-like mouth. Pilots need to examine their ships for mynock infestations, as the creatures like to affix to starships and chew on their power cables. Mynocks travel in packs and typically grow to be 1.6 meters long with a wingspan of approximately 1.25 meters.

SPACE SLUG
Space slugs are colossal, worm-like creatures that reside within the furrows and craters of asteroids and airless planetoids. The slug's bizarre biology allows it to survive in the vacuum of space. Space slugs have been seen to grow up to 800 meters in length. The chaotic Hoth asteroid field is known to host such a massive specimen.

WAMPA
The bone-chilling cold is not the only danger that awaits a traveler on the Hoth plains. Despite standing over two meters in height, the wampa ice creature is nonetheless a stealthy predator. Its white fur is the perfect camouflage, and the howling Hoth winds mask its approach until it is too late. With a crushing blow from its clawed hand, a wampa is strong enough to snap the neck of even a hardy tauntaun.

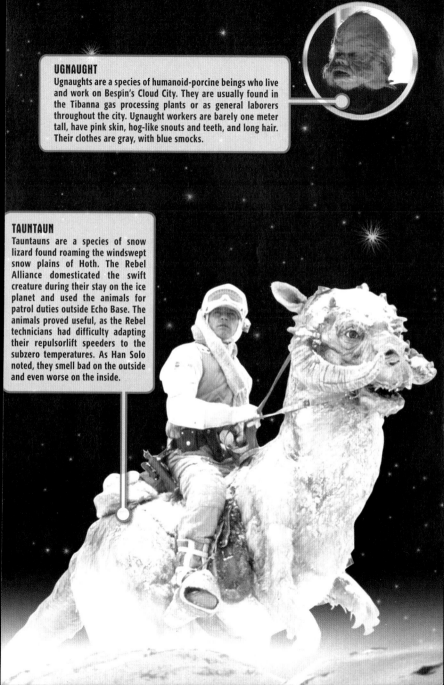

UGNAUGHT

Ugnaughts are a species of humanoid-porcine beings who live and work on Bespin's Cloud City. They are usually found in the Tibanna gas processing plants or as general laborers throughout the city. Ugnaught workers are barely one meter tall, have pink skin, hog-like snouts and teeth, and long hair. Their clothes are gray, with blue smocks.

TAUNTAUN

Tauntauns are a species of snow lizard found roaming the windswept snow plains of Hoth. The Rebel Alliance domesticated the swift creature during their stay on the ice planet and used the animals for patrol duties outside Echo Base. The animals proved useful, as the Rebel technicians had difficulty adapting their repulsorlift speeders to the subzero temperatures. As Han Solo noted, they smell bad on the outside and even worse on the inside.

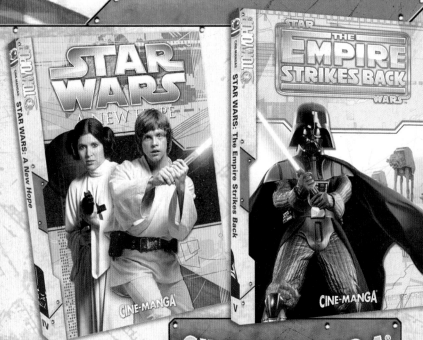

STAR WARS

Coming to the Cine-Manga® Galaxy!

CINE-MANGA®

CLONE WARS

The Clone Wars are
spreading like a fire
across the galaxy

**now in
stores**